Dean Ha

TRAPPED IN ROBLOX!

Dean Hanson

Sconnie Books

Dean Hanson – Trapped In Roblox!

Cover design by: Dean Hanson

For more information, address:
damien@damienhansonbooks.com

FIRST EDITION

ISBN: 9798789299357

Thanks to my Dad for
helping me make my books.
Thanks To A.E. Pole for
helping edit my work.
Thanks to my Mom for
staying up late to watch
movies with me sometimes.
Merry Christmas, Grandma, I
hope you like this present!
And thanks to all of you, my
readers, for letting a kid have
a chance to tell you stories. I
hope you all enjoy it!

Dean Hanson – Trapped In Roblox!

> By shifting your focus to the princess and treating your life's challenges like video games, you can trick your brain and actually learn more and see more success.

> \- Mark Rober

Dean Hanson – Trapped In Roblox!

Contents

FOREWORD

Thanks for reading my book. I tried to write it well and it was a hard time because school started up again and between homework and other studies I wasn't prolific. But I finished it a few days after Christmas, then I made pictures for it so it can look nice.

Please review my book if you like it. It would make me very happy. And you can check out my other book Spider Nightmare Apocalypse on Amazon if you'd like to read my other stuff!

Now on to the story!

Chapter 1 - Computer Shenanigans

It was a stormy night in Korea. Thunder boomed like TNT. Lightning flashed across the sky. It was a scary time in the Hanson household, especially since the thunder reminded me of a thousand a-bombs exploding across the entirety of my hometown.

Things might have been better if it wasn't for the fact that I was in my house alone.

Well, kinda.

My Mom and Dad were sleeping and without them there to give me hugs, I was scared of the constant lightning.

Still, even though it was scary, I realized something brilliant about this stormy night. With my parents sleeping, it could also be a game night!

You see, my parents usually just let me play an hour of computer per day unless

I have friends over or unless it is a special day. But now, with them asleep, they couldn't tell me no.

But I asked anyway. I went to their door and I asked them.

"Can I play on the computer? If you don't want me to play on the computer, just say something. And if you don't say something then I will know that you are okay with me playing on the computer."

I listened, but all I could hear besides the thunder outside was the even louder snoring of my mom. That meant that I could play on the computer!

I tiptoed away from their room and into the computer room. Then I silently closed the door, and I turned my computer on. This was going to be fantastic!

I turned it on, but something wasn't right. The power button was glowing a rainbow color, and when my screen got to Windows there were a bunch of little Roblox figures dancing on my screen!

That was super weird, but I remembered before that my dad said sometimes strange programs get downloaded and installed to your computer if you aren't careful. I made a note to have him check it out the next day.

I grabbed the mouse and tried to move it around, but the mouse pointer was stuck under a big fat Roblox man, and I saw it struggle but it couldn't move. I pulled it right, and it slid out from under the guy. But then he punched it and it flew across my screen and slapped into the edge of Windows. It slid down to the bottom and looked all crumpled and dazed.

I felt bad for the little guy. And also very confused. When had my computer come alive?

Enough was enough.

I ducked under my desk and went through my computer cables. They were all different though. The first one that I grabbed was much longer than I remembered it ever being.

Also, it was transparent, and I could see a subway train running through it.

There were crazy characters sitting in seats throughout the train, and when they all saw Giant me looking at them, they screamed. I apologized and put the cord down.

I picked up a different cord and saw that it was inflating and deflating in a rhythm not unlike the beating of a heart.

That was scary.

I dropped it in an instant and got out from under my desk. This was a mystery that might be very dangerous, and I was determined to go get my mom and dad for help.

But the world outside had different ideas for me.

Do you know what a proton warhead is? It's something I learned about watching sci fi movies and animations, and let me tell you something about them. They explode louder than anything else in the universe. Even louder than nuclear bombs.

Even louder than my mom's snoring.

You know, the kind of snoring that can shake a jetliner out of the sky. The kind that armies around the world want to weaponize and use against their enemies.

Well, the last stroke of thunder that I heard that night was louder than all of that. And it wasn't just loud, it came with color too. A melted golden blue that shot through the walls of the apartment, bathing everything in its light.

I fell over and from the floor I caught a glimpse of my computer. My jaw dropped and I shielded my eyes.

The whole computer was lit up like it was on fire and it blazed a golden yellow and a spectral blue.

I grabbed my smartphone and I dialed the public emergency number, hoping against hope that I could get through to the police and that they could help me before the computer went nuclear and exploded me into dust.

But the call didn't go through.

In fact, I didn't have any service! I sucked in a breath and hoped against hope that I'd survive what came next.

There was an explosion, lots of smoke, and the brightest light that I ever saw. I saw the light and went crazy.

I screamed and even though I knew it was too late for me, I hoped that help could come before the rest of the building went up in flames because of my possessed computer. I closed my eyes and let myself go.

It was time to meet my maker.

The next thing I knew, I opened my eyes and I saw that I was in a starless void. A void that was entirely white with bright light that seemed to shine from the air itself.

I thought I was going to die because to be honest it looked like I might be inside the sun. But I wasn't burning and I didn't get crushed.

Instead I fell for what felt like forever. Right up until I noticed a gray one peg lego box was falling with me. I grabbed onto it and for some reason I stopped falling and started floating as if the lego box was an anti-gravity device.

The white light became a login screen. Words boomed out. "Chingoo2011, would you like to log in?"

"Yes!" I yelled, and then I got dizzy and I blacked out.

Chapter 2 - The Train

I woke up on a train.

Which was weird because I hadn't gone to sleep in one.

The last thing I knew, everything had been all blurry and bright, and I was maybe in the computer? There had been a Roblox log-in screen, hadn't there?

It was a little hard to remember.

All I knew for sure that things here weren't nearly as strange as things had been there.

For one thing, I was sitting in a chair. That was normal. It was a two seater and looking around I saw that the train car was full of them. They were blue leather with red stripes across them, a cup holder on the right side, with unfoldable tray tables in their front.

My tray table was across my lap and it had a white porcelain plate on it, holding a hamburger. Floating above this very plain hamburger was a menu. On it were a ton of options.

I could have a triple cheeseburger, a bacon cheeseburger, a quadruple patty burger — there were so many choices!

And to the right of it all was a sky blue button labeled Customize! I waved my finger at it and a whole new menu opened up. Now my burger could be anything that I wanted.

I could even replace my patties with pancakes!

Or a Tyrannosaurus Rex Burger.

A Booger and Snot Burger.

A super duper extra crispy chicken cheese beef and goat burger.

The sky was the limit.

I could imagine having a burger tower by myself, something so tall that it went to space. And it would make me fatter than the fattest person in the world!

Every morning I could wake up and eat my bed.

That was fun but all I really needed was some chicken and beef in my burger. I couldn't imagine having a beef patty burger with like ten patties.

"Tickets please!" a voice rang out.

I swung my head around in surprise. Did I have a ticket?

The person who was coming kinda freaked me out. He was bald, his shoulders were really wide, and his head was symmetrically round.

He was a Roblox man!

"Tickets please!"

I reached down to my pockets only to notice that I didn't have pockets. It was then that I noticed that my hands weren't hands. They were strange little fingerless nubs.

"Ahhhh!" I screamed. I heard a shriek and some stomping and I turned my head to see the ticket man running out of the train car.

I guess my scream scared him. Oh well, he could do whatever he wanted.

I needed to figure out what was going on. I thought about Roblox and how it all worked and then I imagined that there were a bunch of square boxes in row at the bottom of my vision.

I looked left and right and there they were! They followed wherever I went. In my first box was a train ticket. In the second was five robux. Interesting. And good to know.

I stood up and looked all around me, getting an idea of everyone who was there in the train car with me.

There were gray-skinned Robloxian guests, wearing black shirts and black caps.

There were the regular player Robloxians who had many different shades of skin and lots of varieties of clothing.

And there were different types of strange monsters and other creatures. But none of them were scary.

One of them was even reading a newspaper!

Well this was officially strange, as if it hadn't already been. I decided to get up and check out the whole train. I figured that I better learn as much about this place as necessary.

I walked through a few sleeper cars, with doors to rooms that I bet were quite blocky and small.

I passed by a bathroom, where I could hear the voice of the ticket man telling himself to be brave and calm.

Then I got to the front of the train. And wow was that a sight to see!

The front of the train looked like the long rectangular hood of a cyber truck, with a strangely angular shape that resembled a triangle on top of a square and rounded edges.

The sides of the train were very sleek and from where I was the buildings whizzed by so fast that I could see we were going faster than a bullet.

The land around the track was beautiful. It was a deep fresh green of tall grass in-between farmer fields filled with tan stalks of sweet corn. Between those zipped small forests absolutely teeming with animals of all kinds.

The train was going super fast but in between the blur going past my window I could occasionally see strange animals.

Once I saw ten rather cute squirrels smiling and nibbling on large, brown nuts. If I hadn't known better, I'd say they were waving to me.

Then, my jaw dropped! There were twenty bushy-tailed tiger-sheep outside my window. I didn't think that was possible!

A bell rang. Ding ding ding! The intercom came on again. The voice said, "Our train has arrived at Roblox Central Station Line Five. Please depart. This is the last stop."

The last stop? Oh no! I couldn't just ride it in a loop to get back home?

That was a scary thought. I got in line with the other Robloxians and filed off of the train, then looked around the platform. What was I going to do now?

There were Robloxians of every walk of life here. I could see businessmen who carried briefcases that quite obviously didn't open.

There were train personnel running about, checking trains and changing places with workers.

And in the corner of the first platform I could see a dealer. How did I know that he was a dealer? Well, he had a sign with an arrow pointing at him.

That was good. A dealer was a Robloxian who collected stuff. Often stuff that people didn't actually use, to be honest.

Which was strange and funny.

A dealer would be able to give me something useful or else the dealer could trade me some serious cash.

I was feeling a bit better. All I needed to do was find some good stuff to sell and then I would have the money I needed to get myself out of here!

If I was lucky there'd be something right here at the terminal. I checked the place out, scoping it from where I stood. It was Massive with a capital M — I don't think I ever saw anything so wide and long in my life.

Well, the airport at Incheon maybe, but have you ever seen a train station as big as an international airport? Neither have I.

There were tons of trains all over the place, and so many different tracks and platforms to various destinations. It felt like its own world in so many ways.

Especially since a lot of the trains themselves were quite exotic and new.

The trains were of various and strange sizes and shapes.

There were tiny little trains, maybe mice could ride on them. I am sure I could not fit in one of them without something like a shrink ray.

But then, towering over them, there were gigantic trains that looked like space ships. I could imagine thousands of passengers flying to their destination at close to the speed of light!

The variation was mind boggling!

Looking it all over, it felt like something that you would only see on Earth in the future. There was no way I should be seeing anything like this in the present. But here I was.

Unfortunately, though, I didn't see any thicc loot that I could pick up and sell to the dealer. It looked like I was going to have to figure out a different way.

I started to walk along the main aisle of the station while reading all of the signs to see where the trains were going. There had to be some sort of clue there, something useful that would help me.

I saw one train platform that was full of Robloxians who were dressed in white and had wings and halos. That sign said they were going to Roblox Heaven.

The next one up was full of red Robloxians who had tails, horns and pitchforks. Their sign said they were going to Roblox Hell.

The next one up said the moon, and all of the people there were giant mouse

Robloxians. I guess maybe the Roblox Moon was made of cheese?

And then I had to stop walking because the last platform in that direction was way too hot to get close too. Bright also. I narrowed my eyes and just barely made out the sign.

It said Roblox Sun. Go figure.

I turned around and went the other direction.

After passing the platforms I had seen already I came upon a bunch of new ones.

One said that it was a platform that goes back in time. I think it's for random strangers that accidentally made it in here but from a time that was long ago? There was a dirty caveman standing on the platform and he was hitting the train with his club while Roblox police were trying to shove him into the train.

He kept yelling, "Ooga! Ooga booga!"

I don't know how he got here, I mean, I came by my computer and there is no way that guy had a computer. Unless it was maybe made by some future time traveling computer salesman? I'd have to think about all of that later.

Next was a platform that went into the future. It was like the platform that goes back in time but this one had a man with three arms and nuclear burned clothing hitting the train with his club while shouting "Booga ooga! Ooga!".

The Robloxian police were trying to shove him onto his train and I have to say that seeing him made me a little worried because what the heck happens to Earth in the future?

That was a little bit scary and it made me hope that there were other dimensions as well.

And then I found my destination.

The name of the platform was Dean's Computer and it was super new and shiny like it had just been built.

I wondered if there were other people's computers here too because it didn't feel fair that only I would get a station.

But it didn't feel very unfair a moment later, after I mounted the platform and went to the ticket machine to buy a ticket home.

The machine said that it cost five thousand robux to get there!

That made no sense. Why would it be so expensive!

First I was angry and I kicked the machine.

Then I was sad. There was no way home. I sat on one of the platform's white plastic benches and I put my face in my stubby roblox hands.

What was I going to do?

"Hey, buddy, do you have a ticket?"

I looked up into the face of a Robloxian police officer. He was carrying a truncheon and he didn't look happy at all.

"Oh, sorry," I said and I got off the platform and just started walking. But I didn't go far before I saw something that might be helpful.

There was a sign that said, "Robux Games Lobby - Free Transport every day 6am to 11pm" and I had a feeling that maybe, just maybe, I could find some help there.

I climbed up the platform and pushed myself through the crowd of excited Robloxians that I found there.

And then I waited.

The electronic train ticker said it was coming in ten minutes and I hoped that when I got to my destination I could find the answer that I was looking for.

Chapter 3 - Pay to Play

The train pulled up and screeched to a stop. This one had a gigantic plough in front. It made me wonder what sort of stuff it might run into . . . and through. I mean, why would a train need a plow?

The train's doors opened up and a bunch of Robloxians got out. Then I got in with the mess of people that I had been standing with. Moments later the doors closed and the train lurched forward, pulling out of the station.

The train was large. And when I was leaving I saw something that might be why the plough was in front of the train. There were trees that had fallen and there were lots of those trees laying on the tracks. Which meant that it would be a bumpy ride.

And it was. We smashed through the trunks easily, and the train hopped and sparked, but kept its place upon the tracks.

Out the window I could see that unlike that first train I had ridden this one was moving much more slowly and carefully. And I could see why.

We were riding through a forest.

Trees upon trees were the only thing I could see and I understood why the people in the train ignored the view.

I heard one of the passengers mutter about the trees and then another and another as we bumped and broke through some more trunks.

It was a crazy place to be, the angry muttering rose and I felt like I was in a meeting of the tree haters club.

We smashed through a particularly large chunk of trees and we all heard the snap and tear of metal. Sparks began to fly from the front of the train. The plough had started to get loose! And there were too many trees coming our way.

I heard a cracking sound and I saw the plough clang to the side of the track. We passed by it at a snail's pace.

Now the train was taking some hits and every time it hit a new trunk it cracked and smoked. I looked around, scared, but nobody seemed to care.

Fire started in the front engine and I looked around again, freaking out. But again, no one seemed to mind.

"Are there any firefighters here? Oh my god, we are all going to die!" I yelled. And then the train pulled into the station and the doors opened. I got off as fast as I could. "You guys are nuts!" I yelled.

A Robloxian woman grabbed my arm. Her hair was pink and purple, and she was wearing a sparkly blue jumpsuit. "Come on," she said. "Let me help you out before you get yourself punched out."

She pulled me through the crowd and out of the station, into a cute little park. There was a fountain in the middle and lots of fun playground equipment strewn between the trees. She took us directly to a picnic table and we sat down together.

"Alright, hi. I'm Jelly Janny and it looks like you are not from around here. Either that or you are crazy. Who are you? Where are you from? What are you doing here? Why are you so rude? And how do you plan to do anything while acting like a crazy person?"

"My name is Dean and I need help because I am not from around here and I need to get back home." I said. "I found the train that goes back to my house but it costs five thousand robux to get on it."

Jelly Janny nodded. "That is very expensive. How did you get here in the first place?" she asked. "You probably shouldn't have come here if you didn't have the money to go back."

"I was playing roblox and suddenly my computer started going crazy and this happened," I said.

"But how did you manage to get on the train?" she asked.

"I don't know but after I got into Roblox by my computer I then woke up on a train and this happened because I transferred trains and now I am here" I said.

Jelly Janny put her hand on her chin. "Hmm," she said. "Well, bruh, if you go over to the job center you can be a janitor. That'll get you 1 robux a day so that means you can go home in five thousand days!"

I shook my head. "No, that's a lot. Way too much actually. I was kinda hoping to get home before my parents woke up."

Jelly nodded and she swept her hand around her, pointing at the world of Roblox. "Well, kid, welcome to Roblox. Here you gotta spend money to make money."

I was confused. Spend money to make money? "Are you saying that I can buy money?"

"No, silly. I am saying that you can get robux by spending robux if you have some."

I looked at her with wide eyes. "I have five robux if that's enough," I said. "So now what?"

Jelly grabbed me by the hand and we started walking out of the park. "Let me tell you, buddy boy. That's enough to do one small one, but if you can win then you can do a bigger one and a bigger one."

"A bigger what? What's going on?" I was so confused.

"A game contest of course. Good grief, where are you from again? Nevermind. It doesn't matter. What we have to do is find one you can afford, and then you will have to compete and win."

"Well, I mean I am good at games," I said.

"I sure hope so, Dean, because if you aren't, you are going to be here for a long time." Jelly brought them out of the park and to a booth that said Information in big white letters on top of it. Behind the counter was a super weird-looking giant white head with holes for eyes.

"Ah!" I screamed.

Jelly just looked at me and sighed. "Are you sure you can win game tournaments? Nevermind. Don't answer that. We'll see soon enough." She turned to the giant head. "Hey James, what are the games?"

"How many robux?" The giant head growled slowly. Like super slowly, almost as if he were half-asleep.

"Five."

"That's not many robux," he muttered. His eyes flashed for a few seconds. "Gabriel's Horrendous Obby. Entry fee, five robux. The winning prize is one hundred robux. Go to line seven. It is the third stop."

"Thanks James. Time to find fames!"

I stared at her and cocked my head. "Fames? Really?"

She giggled. "Let's just go. Shall we? You got a game to play and I've got a hankering for a good seat in the stadium and some popcorn!"

Chapter 4 - The Train to the Obby Madness

Jelly Janny and I took the train to Gabriel's Horrendous Obby. It was another bullet train, super fast and packed with excited people. We just barely managed to push our way to a couple of empty seats before they were all full.

"What do we do on this train?" I asked.

"Just sit here. What do you do on trains?" I looked at her closely to see if she was joking but she looked serious. "I don't know. Talk with my dad I guess."

Jelly Janny's mouth dropped open. "You have a dad? I didn't know we could have dads! How many robux did he cost? Does he count as a pet or something? Do you keep him in your inventory?"

I laughed. "No, nothing like that. I mean back home I have a dad and when

I ride the train it is always with him. We talk and play games and stuff."

Jelly Janny looked even more confused. "How do you play games on a train? Is there a game zone in the train?"

"No, we do word games. Sometimes it is guessing animals using the ABCs. Sometimes we do math games where he asks me math questions and I have to tell him the answer. Or we do trivia stuff too."

"Hmm. Doesn't sound explodey enough to be fun for me. But whatever. I'm all about thrills and giggles in a game zone, but when I am on a train I just wait. We can take our time sitting here till we get to the obby," she said. "Oh, you know what? We can eat something. That will be fun. Yeah! I think we should get something to eat or drink."

I looked around the train. I didn't see any restaurants, though to be honest I hadn't expected any. I turned back to Jelly. "How?"

"By waiting for another five . . . four . . . three . . . two . . . one . . ."

The door to the train car opened and a man in a clown suit wearing a king's crown yelled out, "Hey, who's hungry?" The people cheered and a little menu popped up in front of me with all sorts of food items on it.

"Well, what do you want?" she asked.

"I want a triple cheeseburger," I said.

"That's a lot of food. I think I'll just have a coke," she said. My cheeseburger appeared in front of me and Jelly Janny eyed it hungrily. "Scratch that. One triple cheese burger and a coke, please," she said. "Man, I can't wait to have it."

I ate and Jelly Janny drank her coke. But it was super slow. I was surprised. Usually when I have a coke I am done with it in under a minute.

"Are you sipping? How can you even do that?" I asked. She shrugged, then shoved her triple cheeseburger down her throat in 3 seconds flat.

"What are you?" I asked. She smiled, clicked her menu, and another triple cheeseburger appeared. That one was gone in five. "Sorry. My mouth is big so I eat it kind of quickly." I laughed.

Jelly let out a big burp and I did too. Other people on the car turned to glare at us but we didn't care.

"Now, Dean, this is important. You are about to spend all of your money on the upcoming game. Have you played obbies before? Do you know what they are and what to expect?"

"I've tried lots of obbies before with my friend. So I am pretty talented at playing obbies. Sometimes they are too easy," I said.

She rolled her eyes.

"Boys always talk like that. But yeah, if you are telling the truth then you might be good at this. Be careful though, this is a paid obby. That means it's super hard. Because only 0.1% of the people who challenged this obby completed it," she said.

That was news to me. I had never done an obby that was paid, so she maybe had a point. "What sort of traps are there in Gabriel's Horrendous Obby?" I asked.

"Oh there are quite a lot. It's actually a big part of the fun and what makes it so horrendous! Let's see . . . so there are lasers, sawblades, many different kinds of automated gun turrets, teleporters, spikes, boulders, bombs, monsters, and swords. They are hilarious for us in the audience to watch, but they are quite rough on the players because if I remember right there are three hundred levels and only three checkpoints."

"Only three checkpoints!" I exclaimed.

"Yep. When you die you spawn back at the last one you crossed and I don't think I have to tell you how many people that has pulled from first place to last." She put up her boxy roblox hand and poked at it as if she were counting ideas. "I think that's it. Is there anything else you need to know?"

I shook my head slowly. "Bruh, why does there have to be so much chaos?"

She giggled. "You're funny. Of course it has to be chaotic because it's challenging, and that makes it hard. What, would you expect a game with a money prize at the end to be easy?"

I shrugged. In a perfect world it would be.

"Well, I guess this is a good test of my abilities. I need to make a lot of robux and I'll probably have to go hardcore before I can make five thousand robux," I said. "It'll be hard but sometimes you have to just go for it."

"I hope you can do it. I don't know if you can though because it's super tough beating the challenge," she said.

"Thanks for your vote of confidence." She stuck out her tongue at me.

"Just relax," she said. "Here, let me close the curtains and I'll keep watch for the stop. You just take a nap and save up your energy for the obby. It's going to be a hard one."

I didn't think I would be able to fall asleep. I'm not good at it and I hate to do it. Not this time, though.

I suddenly felt so tired and I felt my eyes closing.

I looked over at Jelly and saw that she was asleep. I felt like I should say something but my tiredness was just too strong and soon I was in the land of dreams.

Chapter 5 - Entering a Horrendous Obby

I got off at the station and saw that it was packed with people. There were banners of so many different colors hanging here and there, and I saw that a lot of people were wearing t-shirts with the names and faces of various Roblox gaming stars and youtubers.

There was the purple and pink of "Just Game It In", the mighty orange and red of "Nightmare", the grey and metallic silvers of "TechnoSword", it was a gala of who's who in the gaming world and here I was standing and breathing in the middle of it all.

People were chanting the names of their favorites, others were yelling mean things like "Noobs!" and "Go Home! Nobody wants you here!"

Overall it was a dazzling experience. I stood and stared, and Jelly Janny had to grab my arm and pull me along to get me out of there.

"Why are there so many people?" I asked.

It turned out that she didn't have to answer because as soon as we exited the station I could see why.

This place was amazing!

It was a slapdash smorgasbord of bizarre buildings colored in every color from the rainbow, strung with festive Christmas lights. The mess of people made a buzzing noise as they talked and chattered, so many words in such a small place that it was almost impossible to actually know what any of them was saying.

Jelly Janny studied my face and broke into a wide grin.

"Welcome to Yoonstown, home of Gabriel's Horrendous Obby. Home to a lot of stuff actually," she said, gesturing all around.

There were huge clothing stores filled with the latest and greatest in Roblox attire.

There were strangely narrow and tall emoticon stores that let you grandstand during battle matches.

There were even stores for new body parts and heads.

I know this was Roblox world but those stores still seemed strange and creepy. Imagine walking past a store filled with faces and you'll know what I mean!

"So what do we do now?" I asked.

Jelly swept her hand over and pointed down the street.

"It's been a while since I've been here, to be honest, but I think we go straight, then take a right at Turtle Street and then a left on Meoni. And the stadium will be straight ahead."

We walked through the crowds of crazy Roblox characters, ducking under flying pets, and dodging the brims of comically wide hats until, finally, we were at our destination.

Gabriel's Horrendous Obby. It looked massive and even from the outside I could see the levels rising up into the heavens.

"Woah!" I exclaimed.

Jelly Janny giggled.

"Come on," she said, grabbing my hand and pulling me with her.

There was a huge line at the front doors but Jelly took me around to a different side that had a small wooden door, the sign "competitors-only", and no line at all. She knocked on it and a slot opened within it.

"Whaddya want?" the voice said. He sounded like a chimpanzee if chimpanzees could talk.

"We are here for the competition," Jelly said. "I'll take a VIP visitors pass for me and he'll take a registration ticket please."

There was the sound of a shuffling of papers and a little cough. "Does he got the Robux?"

I handed my five robux to Jelly Janny and watched it disappear into the little slot. Well, I was in it now. Two passes came out, a yellow visitor's pass for her and a sky blue competitor's pass for myself. I grabbed it and it appeared in my Roblox slot inventory as item number one.

The door popped open and sure enough, the ticket man was a chimpanzee. He waved us through a dark hallway and we walked for a bit before it opened up into a room full of other people with light-blue passes.

"Well that is my cue. Good luck! See ya at game time. I'll be cheering for you!" Jelly said. And she left the room, going through a yellow door on my right.

A different door, a light blue one, opened up and a man stuck out his head.

"Ten minutes to crunch time," he said.

I looked around at the other competitors, confused. But they all seemed to know what it meant so I decided I would just follow their lead. There was a set of stairs that led to a viewing window so I went up those and took a look at what I was going to be facing.

And my eyes widened. What I saw was terrifying because there were so many weapons.

In the first few levels all I could see between jumps and speed ramps were lasers.

Big lasers, small lasers and a single laser minigun.

It looked scary but I'd done a lot of obbies before as a player and I knew they were more bark than bite.

At level ten I saw that there was a boss you had to get passed and that I wasn't used to. He was a knife-wielding robot three times as big as any of us here and he stomped, jumped and kicked in a way that looked really tough to beat.

Past him I saw there were escape rooms full of lava and electric flooring, then levels filled with saw blades and at the farthest ones in sight I saw rows and columns filled with flamethrower traps.

If this was a hitpoint-based game then the fire wouldn't be such a problem. But in an obby that was one shot then one kill, the way it spread into the shape of a triangle made it into a big problem.

I tore my eyes away from the levels and took a moment to scan the bleachers.

There sat a huge audience of so many types and shapes of Robloxians all waving and cheering even before the event had begun.

The stadium seating floated in rings around the game levels and I immediately understood that as us runners went up the levels, the stadium would follow us. I was impressed.

These Robloxians had thought of everything!

All at once my knees felt like jelly and I knew I wasn't ready and that I would fail. I wanted to walk out the way I had come in.

If I failed, it would take me a long time to go home.

And worse than that, I knew that if I failed here and now where it was most important not to, in my mind I would fail forever.

Jelly Janny had wished me good luck. Plus she didn't seem too worried. Maybe she thought I could do it.

If she thought I could, maybe it was really possible?

I looked through the audience and I saw her sitting there munching on popcorn. She was holding a little flag that they must have made at the last minute in the local shop because it had my name and my face on it.

That sealed the deal.

I was going to run this obby and I was going to win.

Chapter 6 - The Obby

There were one-hundred of us at the starting line, three-hundred stages until the finish line, and one-hundred robux to be won. Around us floated the stadium, full of cheering fans. A man with a checkered white and black shirt held a flag and stood at the side of the starting line.

"Ready, Set, Go!" the man yelled. He waved his flag and we all ran forward. But it wasn't long before a group of six of them moved over to me and boxed me in. One was in front of me, another one was behind me, and there were two on each side of me.

"Lucky me," I muttered.

The one in front of me sneered and slowed way down. "Boss says he don't like the look of you. And you know what? I don't like the look of you either," he said.

The rest of the Robloxian thugs laughed, but it was evil and forced.

The guy in front of me was looking over his shoulder at me. The guys to my sides were looking sideways.

So they didn't notice the sudden appearance of a row of spinning saw blades coming up from the ground in front of us all.

"BZZZZ!" they sounded, and only me and the thug behind me jumped up and over them.

"Have fun catching up!" I yelled back toward the start line where they had just reappeared. I hooted and sped up.

This was going to be a lot of fun.

"Hey, get back here!" yelled the last guy.

He was trying to catch me, but I was faster than him. Three orbs of light circled down from above and started firing pink laser bolts at the runners. Ten of them disappeared back to the start while we all dodged, jumped and weaved. One of those ten was my bad guy.

"Sayonara, sucker!" I said as he screamed and disappeared.

Now it was me and eighty-five others.

Not a bad start. I was surprised at how bad the goons had been at the obby and I wondered which of the runners was their boss.

I couldn't think for long though.

Holes started appearing at random in the running track and I stopped looking over, focusing on jumping and dodging to get to the next stage.

All eighty-five of us blazed across thirty stages in the next five minutes.

The stadium rockets roared as the crowds followed us up, screaming and waving flags. I saw Jelly Janny standing up and hopping up and down, popcorn flying all around her from her popcorn bag as if it were some sort of tasty volcanic eruption, and it made me happy.

This was a lot of fun!

As we progressed, things got harder.

The track sloped up so that we were running up a hill, and giant spiked metal balls came rolling down them. The first took out twelve people. The second took out nine.

When we got to the top of the hill, some of the other runners screamed. Standing in front of us was the giant robot boss. It was stomping and waving its arms about, shooting saw boomerangs, and trying to make it impossible for us to get past.

"This might not have been a good idea!" I yelled out loud.

Some of the other runners nodded their blocky heads. That robot looked annoyingly difficult and I wasn't sure what any of us could do.

Then I saw something that I hadn't expected.

As we all got close one of the Roblox guys, a black-haired guy whose name showed as EVILDOOD in white letters above him, shoved another one into the robot and then ran around the robot when it smashed the guy!

"Bruh!" I yelled. "Totally uncool!"

The evil Roblox man saluted me with fingerless hands and I watched him run off. The other runners had stopped and weren't sure what to do. But then I had an idea.

"Hey everyone, this looks impossible but there has to be a trick. It doesn't look right. I think maybe because it is so big we all have to slide under it at the same time. It won't know where to stomp and then we can all get past him and get that bad guy!"

The other runners nodded. "Three . . . Two . . . One . . . Go!" I said.

All of us ran at the robot. It lifted up a giant blocky foot and as one we dove and slid past him. His foot stayed up, the robot unsure of who to stomp and as I got back up I saw he was stuck that way, smoke now coming out of his robot head.

I had killed the robot! I laughed. This was amazing.

But EVILDOOD was still far ahead. I saw him in the distance dancing past spots of lava and acid.

At this rate he was going to win!

The thought made me very angry. I ran as fast as I could forward. Giant laser beams started flashing out from the air, coming at us from all angles. A bunch of runners disappeared but I stayed my lane, rolling under one laser and jumping over another.

The crowd went wild and a video screen appeared in the light blue Robloxian sky showing me doing my thing. Above it flashed the words, "**New Game Run Speed Record - Laser Lobby Attack!**" Above that showed a leaderboard and a position log.

I was second in the race and eighty-nine stages in. That meant that there was a checkpoint coming soon.

The number changed and I was suddenly in third place. Over me in the sky someone was clipping in and out of existence, flying and laughing. "Hacker!" I exclaimed, shaking my fist.

Another figure appeared. A bearded flying giant. And he was carrying a hammer. The word "Ban" was written on its side. In a flash of a moment he smacked the cheating guy and I was back in second. I breathed a sigh of relief.

"Oh, ok, I guess that works," I said.

Behind me whoever was in third place laughed at my joke. But a second later he stopped laughing as a bunch of turrets popped out of the ground and started firing.

This was suspicious.

I could see EVILDOOD out in front of us and I know he didn't get any turrets. What was going on?

Chapter 7 - An Identified Agent

I juked and the third place runner took a bullet meant for me, disappearing to the start of the race. More bullets flew and I knew, if I looked behind me, there wouldn't be a lot more runners left.

But as suddenly as it had all started, it stopped and I was through.

"EVILDOOD, you cheater, how didn't you get shot by the turrets?" I screamed ahead.

I heard evil chuckling, but no answer. It was alright, though. As I ran forward I found that if I stayed in a straight line my speed increased.

Keeping my eye on EVILDOOD, I ran in a straight line and soon I was zipping forward so fast that I didn't even have to jump the huge gaps at the end of each stage.

It was like I was hacking. But I wasn't. I was exploiting instead.

The crowd oohed and aahed while EVILDOOD kept running a zig-zag pattern so that he could keep an eye on me.

"How are you doing that?" he asked as I gained on him. He didn't know the fast run tactic.

Good.

A line of flame shot out and I blazed past at the last second, not getting hit. A series of spike traps tried to break and tip me into their pits, but when they opened I was no longer there.

I was almost to EVILDOOD now and I chanced a look back.

Trailing behind me were some camera drones, their engines whirring hard to try to keep up, and in the far distance were the other runners. They looked like specks, they were so far behind us.

"Let's see how you deal with this," said EVILDOOD when I started to pass him.

A wrench appeared in his hand and he swung out, trying to hit my face. But his wrench met empty air and I was already ahead of him, going faster and faster.

He disappeared behind me and I didn't even bother to look back.

Trap after trap came and I ran in a straight line right past them.

I passed the first checkpoint, then the second. Looking up at the scoreboard I saw that the second best player was on stage 150 and I was on 200.

This was exhilarating.

I laughed, bathed in the excitement of winning and the relief that I would get my much needed cash prize.

"How are you so fast?" a voice yelled from the flying bleachers.

I looked over and there was Jelly Janny, standing up and cupping her mouth to make herself heard.

"A trick I figured out," I answered. "But to be honest my legs feel like they are on fire. Wouldn't it be horrible if they actually were on fire?"

The crowd agreed.

"Wait, what, you can hear me?" I was super confused as the crowd said yes out loud.

"Then what do you think about me going faster than ever?" I said.

"Super cool!" "You're an obby legend" "You're going so fast!" "You will win!" "Yeah!" "Cheer him on guys!" the crowd said.

"Woah thanks" I said.

The crowd was hoping I would win, and my biggest fan was JellyJanny. She started dancing something she called the Dean Dance and soon everyone in her section of the stands was bobbing and weaving, shaking their hips then yelling, "Ooga ooga!"

I was super happy as I reached the end. "The winner is Chingoo2011!" the announcer said on the microphone, calling me by my Roblox Username. "Now the winner will be given 100 robux as promised".

"I beat the obby in 30 minutes," I said.

The crowd was cheering louder than ever. Everywhere I looked I saw Dean flags, Dean T-Shirts and even some crazy guy wearing just a pair of Dean underwear, my face looking at me from the back of his shaking butt.

Where was Jelly Janny? I looked around over the massive crowd and I couldn't see her at all. I bumped fingerless fists with strangers, pushing through the crowd to find my friend.

"Thanks for the big support. If it wasn't for you guys I wouldn't have won! Big thanks to you all!" I said. But I was getting a little worried. Jelly should be here.

The crowd was clapping and whistling and from behind me someone poked me in the back.

"Freeze mister!"

I turned around and I saw Jelly. "Oh my gosh I was so worried! Where were you?"

"I was selling Dean merchandise. I am your agent now." She turned to the crowd. "Step aside, coming through, my boy needs to get himself to the next competition!"

"Go, go! We want to see that," yelled the crowd.

"I do?" I asked.

"You do," she answered. She smiled wide. "And I bet you'll do even better at that one than you did with this one!"

'

As she pulled me through the crowd I let my mind wander. How had I done so well with such an easy trick? Was it because I am a human inside a game?

That race had been super easy. And it wasn't like the Robloxians hadn't been trying. Maybe here I was a superhero in some ways.

It made me confident — I was going to win and keep winning. Nothing was going to stop me from getting out.

Chapter 8 - Tycoon Tyranny

The stadium was very crowded, but Jelly Janny was an expert at pulling me through the crowd. She had set one shoulder hard in front of her and was smashing through everyone unfortunate enough to stand in her way. Her other hand was gripping my ear and pulling me along while I squealed and protested.

"Hey! Ow! Stop it!" I complained. But she was very effective and I couldn't really disagree with her results. We were where she wanted us to be in a very short time.

"We're here," she announced. I looked up. Baskin's Bodacious Buys, the sign said. It was a shop. "Huh?" I asked. "What are we doing here?"

"Buying stuff. Doi. It's on me, by the way, because I made a lot of robux selling Dean merch at that game there. The most popular one was the hoodie with the picture of you doing a T-pose. So here I am going to give you a chance to buy something fun that might help you win me more money at the next game."

I smiled and then paused. "Win you more money?"

"Us," she corrected.

I laughed. Okay, that was fine. But what did I need to buy? The store was gigantic and filled with so many items. There were hoverboards, baseball bats, guns; all sorts of things including Communism?

I wasn't sure what that was but I wasn't about to buy it.

We wandered through the aisles and rows, peering down at price tags and items and getting an idea for something that I might need.

Stores are strange like that.

Somehow you often enter them not needing anything and then when you are there you realize that your life is missing so much stuff.

In my case, I was missing my best teddy friend, Chingoo. He is a big fat sheep and I love him to death.

"Hey, Jelly, is there any way that I can bring someone from the real world into the game world?" I asked.

"Yes. And it'll cost me all of the robux that I made off of your merch, but I have a good feeling about sales at the next game. You can buy a pet ticket," she answered.

I nodded. I wasn't exactly sure what it was but I often got pets when I played

Roblox games. They were super cute and small and they usually floated around like crazy bees on the hunt for pollen.

"Alright, how do we get it?" I asked.

Jelly Janny grabbed me by the ear and started pulling me again.

"Ow! Why!" I complained, but she just shushed me and pulled me through the store to a counter.

"One pet ticket please," she said, slapping one-hundred robux down in front of the cashier.

She had let go of my ear and I watched the whole sale in wonder. It is hard not too when the cashier is a retired scientist who looks exactly like Mark Rober!

"Uh," I said. "Isn't that the retired NASA scientist Mark Rober?"

Jelly Janny put a finger on my lips. "Shhh! You are embarrassing me."

"But, but, Mark Rober!"

"Shush," she said. She took something out of her inventory and suddenly my mouth was a zipper. She closed it and turned back to Mark Rober. "Sorry about that."

Mark Rober laughed. "It's okay. Happens all the time. Here's one ticket. Make sure to click that button and subscribe. And have a great day!"

I unzipped my mouth. "But Mark Rober!"

It was too late. Jelly had me by the ear and soon we were on the streets bashing through crowds of surprised Robloxians on our way to the train station.

I grabbed at my mouth and was surprised when the zipper disappeared and reappeared in my inventory.

Jelly Janny snorted. "Took you long enough! I was wondering when you'd figure out that you could just pocket the zipper. I'm starting to wonder if maybe you aren't as good at this game as you think you are."

I pulled her hand off of my ear. "What are you talking about, you exotic demon!"

She laughed and winked, then grabbed my hand and bashed us the rest of the way to the train station. It was full of people, mostly fans and a lot of them were wearing my merch.

I closed my eyes, waiting for them to recognize me and go crazy. But nothing happened! I opened my eyes and saw that Jelly had put a fake nose, fake mustache and fake glasses on me. No one knew it was me!

She gave me a knowing smile and I took the opportunity to select my pet ticket. There was a spring and a sproing and then there appeared an incredibly fat teddy sheep, Chingoo. He was flying around my head and I had to jump to grab him.

I got him and I gave him a big old hug. Then we headed over to a booth that said Information in big white letters on top of it. It was just like the last one we had gone too. It even had that same crazy looking giant white head with holes for eyes.

"Ah!" I screamed.

Jelly looked at me and rolled her eyes. "Are you going to do that every time we visit the kiosk?"

"Ching!" my teddy sheep said from my arms. "What he said," I answered.

Jelly sighed and turned to the giant head. "Hey James, what are the games?"

"How many robux?" The giant head growled. Super slow, just like before.

"One-hundred."

"That's a good amount of robux," he muttered. His eyes flashed for a few seconds. "Tycoon Madness. Entry fee, one-hundred robux. The winning prize is one thousand robux. Go to line one, it is the tenth stop."

"Thanks James, time to find fames!"

The two of us went a few platforms down and when the train arrived, we got onboard, totally psyched for the coming game.

Chapter 9 - The Tycoon Admins

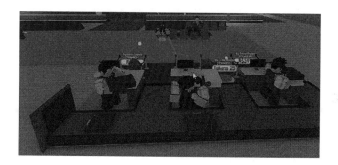

My agent Jelly Janny and I got off the train and we were swarmed by a bunch of fans in a matter of seconds.

"Uh, Jelly, what do we do?" I whispered. "We need to get through here and into the next stadium but there are too many people."

"It's definitely a real mess. Why don't we just go straight there? I know there are probably markets and side quests on the way, and we have time, but I really don't want to deal with all of these people," she answered.

Then we saw the crowd was getting bigger and more people started gathering while other trains were loading off even more fans that knew me. The crowd saw us and they got excited, streaming in and screaming their admiration.

"I can't wait to see your next game!" yelled one lady. "You rock!" yelled another. So excited were they to see the next game, I thought that they might crush us to death before we could get to the next stadium! We pushed through the crowds and through the streets, battling my fans, until a team of swat-dressed Robloxians reached us and made a circle around us.

"Step aside everyone! Dean's got a game to get to!"

My teddy sheep floated lazily around my head and one of the guards pointed an M16 at him. Chingoo squealed in alarm.

"Is that teddy sheep with you?" the guard asked.

"Yes!" I said, grabbing him and putting him back into my Roblox inventory. "Sorry Chingoo, but you are going to have to stay in there for a while. At least until it is safe."

We got to the stadium in record time, and moved past long lines of spectators to another special door made just for us players.

"Ticket please," the guards at the entrance said.

This door wasn't so secretive. It was clear glass with a gray shade to it. And because it was weak, there were four guards in front of it, and some sort of desk with papers on it. The papers looked to be built into the desk, though, because I tried to select them and maybe add them to my inventory and I couldn't.

"Here" Jelly said while getting the ticket out of her item box.

"Thank you," they said.

The door opened and we were waved through. The other guards, the ones with the M16s, they stayed behind and I saw them head back out into the crowds.

I guess there were more gamers who needed to be saved from their fans.

We walked forward, our footsteps echoing across the empty lobby, and I turned to ask Jelly a question but she was staring ahead at something and it kind of put me off.

"Hey Jelly, what are you looking at," I asked her. I had followed her gaze but I couldn't see anything crazy.

"I was just thinking about the kind of game you are about to play. I'm not looking at anything. Are you sure about playing this one? Maybe you should wait a day and take a different type of game. Tycoon games are hard."

I smiled. It made me happy that she was worried about me.

"Jelly, I think this will be easy," I said.

"Are you sure?" she asked. "There are some big names playing here tonight. I saw them on the billboards outside. And if you lose, you will have to start making your money all over again."

I shrugged, my blocky shoulders popping up then down like the start of some sort of goofy emote. "It is too late now anyways. I already bought the ticket to play."

The two of us walked to a door that said 'Gamers Only' and the hallway after sloped down like a backwards ramp. We followed it and soon enough we were in a dark room filled with other competitors.

The place was like a high tech locker room. There were TV screens that resembled windows and they showed us that the crowds were now coming in. The time to play was coming.

"Good luck!" Jelly said and she waved as she left and joined the crowd. The rest of us kinda just walked around, eyeing each other.

They didn't look so tough.

There was one guy in a mouse suit. Another guy was wearing a football jersey and carrying a boombox.

He was annoying because his music was all broken garbage music, and I guessed that he was going to get mobbed in the game.

Most of the rest were just standard builds, no robux spent on clothing or avatar looks. A trumpet sounded, and suddenly everyone was gone and I was in the arena.

The challenge had started. But where was everybody?

The other business plots were there but I didn't see anybody in them.

Had they been sent somewhere else? Were they somehow late?

But then I saw one and then another factory building appear in the lots. In this game we couldn't see what each other were doing until we got outside!

I tried to slap my forehead but instead punched it with my blocky roblox hand, fell over backwards, and saw my 100 hp drop to 99.

Ah crud.

And, outside, I saw one of the factories upgrade to two floors. I was being an idiot and losing!

"CHECK OUT THIS DEAN FELLOW. TALK ABOUT A NOOB!" the game admin announced to the stadium.

"I HOPE NOBODY BET ANY ROBUX ON HIM BECAUSE HE IS GOING TO LOSE. REMEMBER, FOLKS, IN ORDER TO WIN YOU MUST BUILD A FIVE FLOOR FACTORY. THIS GUY WILL BE LUCKY TO GET TO TWO!"

"Yeah I don't really care and stop being mean," I yelled.

And I got into gear.

First I made a very short conveyor belt, then I bought an ore dropper. There was also the option for an ore refiner and I got that too.

I knew that a lot of players in Tycoons go for weapons and fancy looking buildings first, so I figured if I focused on making money, I could still win this thing.

"AND NOOB BOY FINALLY STARTS DOING STUFF. HOW MUCH DO YOU WANT TO BET THAT HE WILL QUIT BEFORE THE GAME EVEN FINISHES?"

I was super mad now. But I didn't answer and just kept working. The short conveyor meant that I was getting cash fast, and I had put it next to the "Bank It" button so that I could keep walking over and saving the money.

If the others raided me they'd be in for a funny surprise because they would find no money here to take.

"HEY NOOB, YOU CAN'T WIN. STOP TRYING!" the admin said.

But then another announcer cut in. "Stop being rude man." This voice wasn't so loud, and it had a nice feel to it. He sounded a lot like my dad, to be honest.

It made me try harder. I lengthened the conveyor and bought more refiners. I knew that I could get production bonuses if I upgraded my facility, but two floors would just make me a target.

I heard lasers and explosions outside of the building and after a minute the two story players building came crashing down. Yep, I nodded to myself. That's what happens.

"I AM NOT RUDE. HE'S JUST A DUMB NOOB. YOU ARE JUST LYING!" the rude admin announced. Apparently, he had just been too surprised to answer before.

"No, shut up. Nobody likes you," the other admin said.

"NO-" the first admin started, but then a third voice broke in. He sounded like Yoda from Star Wars, which was kinda funny.

"Shut up both of you guys should. Fight all of the time you guys should not."

I laughed. That was pretty funny. I wondered if all of this fighting wasn't just part of the entertainment.

I wouldn't let it distract me though. I still had a game to win.

Outside there was the sound of machine gun fire and then a bomb. Another factory jumped to two stories and shortly after that it exploded and fell.

And then it hit me. By staying small and working hard, I was going to win. Because they were all fighting rather than playing!

They were ignoring me, probably because the admin had called me a noob and made fun of me.

I smiled. This was going to get really fun in just a minute.

I added more conveyors, more droppers, more refiners while factories rose and fell outside under swarms of bullets and missiles.

Then I took my massive saving from the "Bank It" button, and I upgraded everything I could.

Second floor? Check.

Missile turrets? Check.

Machine gun turrets? Of course!

I also grabbed armor and spent another 5k on a pistol. It wasn't much of a weapon, but with all of those turrets they weren't going to take out my factory.

I double-checked my income tab and saw that it said 571 per second.

Fantastic.

I could go out, blast some enemies, keep them fighting so that they wouldn't think to increase their money production, and I'd win in no time.

I stepped out of my factory and the other players stared at me in shock. It was the first time they had seen me since the game started and there I was, holding a pistol and flanked by gun and missile turrets.

"Hey guys guess what?" I asked.

"What?" they asked back.

"This noob is going to win."

And I started shooting, targeting them with my pistol and my turrets.

Two of them exploded right away, respawning in their factories, but they ran back out, firing AK-47s at me and my turrets.

I ran sideways and then zig-zagged, avoiding their bullets and killing another player. Behind me the factory dinged and churned, making me more and more money while I fought.

"Let's team him!" one of the players yelled. He was wearing a blue hat with a star on it, and I made sure to remember that so that I could keep blowing him up.

Because teaming was rude.

And probably the only way I could lose at this point.

Four went in one direction and three in the other. I exploded the blue hat guy from the three group and then grabbed 15k from my growing money pile, switching to an Uzi.

Bullets flew past me and one of my turrets exploded. But I returned fire, kicking the other two back to respawn. Then I replaced the broken turret.

"How are you doing that?" blue hat guy asked.

"With good planning," I answered.

I heard an explosion and saw that the other group was attacking the opposite side of my factory, so I ran inside, built more turrets on that end, and spent the rest of my money on as many droppers and refiners as I could.

It was a gamble but my money production shot up to 2000 per second.

"Looks like Dean is a noob after all," the blue hat guy yelled. "When the fighting got hot, he ran away."

I just waited, patiently, watching my money rise.

"Hey chicken, you think we are KFC? Come on out. We just want to play."

I waited a little more, and finally I had it. I spent my money and came out of the factory riding inside of an M1 Abrams Tank.

"AHHHHHHHHHHHH   RETREAT!" the blue hat guy said while running from my very powerful shots and my machine-gun.

All seven players ran into the factory closest to mine. While they ran I secretly upgraded to the minigun inside of my tank and then got out and snuck around to the back.

I heard them inside talking through ways to defeat me. But it was too late for them.

I walked into the factory.

"Hello boys," I said, leveling my minigun. And with a snarl of my bullets, they were gone. A timer chimed and I was the winner!

Chapter 10 - The Peaceful Rest With Jelly Janny

I found Jelly Janny surrounded by a horde of fans.

Some of them were wearing zombie skins!

But even the zombies were wearing my merch. I was happy for her; sales must have been through the roof.

At the moment, though, I needed to break her out of that mess because I was hungry and I bet she was too.

"Hey Jelly, look out!" I said. Then I charged with both of my blocky hands out in front of me. People got knocked down and fell over left and right and I was next to her in no time.

"So, what is a good place to eat at around here?" I asked, pushing her out of the crowd with me. We kept running, a horde of Robloxians chasing behind us to buy more merch. "Also, is there any way that we can maybe lose them?"

Just then we both heard a voice.

"Portals for sale! Get your fresh, glowy portals." We both looked, stunned. There was a guy there and he looked just like Mark Rober!

"Duuuude," I said and Jelly nodded. We ran over to him, the horde of fans screaming at our blocky heels.

"How much?!" Jelly yelled as we got over to him. Roblox Mark Rober looked at us and then at the crowd running behind us.

"Let's say a hundred robux?"

Jelly's face turned beet red. "A hundred? That's all of the money I just made selling Dean merchandise! No way."

"Uh, Jelly Janny?" I asked. I pointed my block hand at the crowd. They were getting very close.

"Fine," she said and she stomped her blocky feet. Mark threw her a portal and she tossed it onto the ground. "Hamster Rick's Hamburgers and Hotdoges please," she yelled. Then the two of us jumped through.

We entered into a sort of wormhole that was made of many shades of blue. It felt like we were levitating, but I could see that we were also falling.

Above us was what looked like a white hole and below us was a black hole.

I wondered if maybe this was what it was like to fall when you were a feather. We were there for about thirty seconds before Jelly hit the black hole, screamed, stretched out like a spring, and then disappeared with a big, wet fart.

I screamed and started trying to swim back upwards.

That did not look fun.

But it was no use. I was stretched and then farted onto the grassy ground next to an annoyed-looking Jelly Janny.

"Mark Rober gave us a very low level portal," Jelly Janny fumed.

I got up and looked around. We were in a giant lobby full of restaurant tycoon customers. I breathed a sigh of relief.

Those nerds didn't care about obbies nor fighting tycoons so they wouldn't know me.

From the center of the lobby grew a giant tree that sparkled and looked like it might be a thousand years old.

Part of the tree was missing, though, and I could see that its wood had been used to make the giant, wide, and white restaurant that dominated this tycoon city.

On the roof of the building was a giant and strong hamster flexing his muscles. Next to him were the neon words, Hamster Rick's Hamburgers and Hotdoges.

"You said doges before and I just thought you were stupid," I said to Jelly Janny. She started to snarl something, but I put up my hand and she stopped. "Hey, hey, no, I am stupid. It really is doges!"

"It sure is," Jelly said. "And they are the best tasting doges in the world."

I was confused. Weren't doges a crypto-coin?

Whatever. It was time to eat.

The two of us walked through the peaceful lobby and to the entrance. There were signs all over the front windows advertising their specials for the day.

One was the quintillion patty challenge. A chain of burgers that, when cooked, reached from here to the moon.

If you could eat them all in ten minutes, you and your friends could eat for free, forever!

I opened my mouth wide at that. How crazy was this place?

Then a bee flew in and the next minute was me just coughing and sneezing and saying very bad words.

"Tsk tsk," Jelly said and laughed. Then we entered the restaurant.

We went to the counter and got a menu. Burgers, fries, fried chicken and drinks were listed.

Plus hamster pellets?

I like to think that I am very open to new food but I wasn't about to try to eat those.

We ended up ordering two triple cheeseburgers, two sodas, and two sets of fries and then we took them to the table.

It was all very delicious.

"Hey Jelly," I asked through a bite of burger. It was kinda hard to talk because in this tycoon every bite of the burger made a loud and high-pitched *yum yum yum* sound. "What do we do next?"

"We should rest. And get ready for the next challenge," she said as she sipped her cola.

I started mowing down the rest of my triple cheese burger because I was really hungry after that match.

"But shouldn't I be trying to get home?" I asked.

Jelly frowned. "Well, I know exactly the next match you should do and you now have just enough robux to do it. But it won't happen for a few hours yet so maybe we should instead ride a train somewhere and have some fun."

I thought about it. It wasn't everyday that someone got to go live in a game and she was right about needing to relax. I finished my burger and accidentally let out a long and large burp.

"Excuse me," I said and Jelly laughed.

We finished up our food and left. The train station wasn't far away and we were there in under five minutes.

Once we got there, though, things got strange. None of the trains were stopping!

Not only that, the trains that were coming through were mostly empty and seemed to be driven by roblox gamers from the server.

"Man, how are we supposed to go anywhere if those trains won't stop here?" I asked.

"I guess we will have to buy a train or something," Jelly said. I stared at her, looking her up and down to see if she was joking.

"You can buy a train? How?"

Jelly Janny giggled. "Oh it's easy, you silly boy. At most stations the trains are public access so you can ride them but you can't drive them. But in special servers like this, the owners like to change the rules a bit. It looks like in this place they want you to buy mini trains if you want to leave by train. Which is pretty neat because we get to drive the train on public tracks! It only costs 5 robux and you get to control them."

I was totally up for it. In fact I could barely contain my excitement!

"Let's do it," I said, hopping up and down before doing a T-pose.

We bought a mini bullet train, a silvered-sleek model that said it could go nine-hundred and ninety-nine miles per hour but could only carry the two of us.

I sat in the driver seat and Jelly sat next to me. The dashboard was all electronics and flashing lights and it looked so complicated.

But Jelly Janny twisted some dials and typed on the keypad and our route was set. I turned up the throttle and the next thing we knew, we were going to a station called Majorly.

We headed there and saw that it was a huge global train depot, but not only was it a depot it was also a train station!

"WOAH" I said out loud. I also saw my fans wearing Dean merch. I was scared because I thought I was going to get crushed like a sandwich again.

"Let's avoid the crowds of fans, ok?" Jelly asked.

I agreed and went to places with the least amount of people. We saw another Mark Rober shop on the way and I tried to stop and shop there.

"MARK ROBER," I moaned when Jelly pushed me past the store.

"We're not going shopping," Jelly sighed.

I looked at her.

"What are we going to do then?" I asked.

"We are going to go to Roblox Land, the best amusement park ever!"

I was confused. She was out of money and I had robux but I couldn't go around spending them like crazy and still be able to afford to enter the last contest.

But then she showed me two entrance tokens and I started grinning like a crazy man.

Free I could afford.

"Well, what are we waiting for? Let's go!" I exclaimed.

We went to a carnival and the next hour and a half was a wonderful time.

Well, except for the rollercoaster. I hated that because I am afraid of heights. But what she had said about relaxing turned out to be exactly right.

We rode the log ride, smashed each other with bumper cars, sped over ramps with golf carts, and just had a wicked and wild time of it.

I even got to eat some cotton candy!

But it was coming time for us to leave and go to the game. I looked back once as we went to the train station, our private train now all used up and gone, and I wondered for the first time if I wouldn't be very happy living here in Roblox land.

Chapter 11 - The Dome

Jelly and I went to the next stadium and it was packed like the last two stadiums. It looked like they came earlier than we did.

"This place is crowded. Like, really crowded. It looks like this is the grand stadium?" I asked.

I didn't hear an answer. I turned and saw Jelly already walking off, probably to sell more Dean merch.

I guess I was on my own.

That was fine. I needed to get to the locker room anyway. It was time to meet the competition. I started walking over, happy to see that no one noticed who I was.

That happiness was short-lived.

Over the speakers came the words of the announcer, echoing like a bad speaker at a McDonald's Drivethrough.

"HELLO EVERYBODY, WELCOME TO GRAND STADIUM, HOME OF THE HARDEST STADIUM OF ALL TIME. OR AT LEAST THAT'S WHAT OUR MERCH SAYS!"

I looked over and saw an angry Jelly Janny shaking her blocky fist at the speaker and I laughed. She didn't like the sales competition I guess.

All around me the crowd cheered.

"CHALLENGERS OR CHAMPIONS, WHOEVER YOU SUPPORT, ALL ARE COMING IN TODAY TO COMPETE FOR THE BIGGEST CASH PRIZE IN THE GAME. A WHOPPING ONE MILLION ROBUX! LET ME HEAR YOU SAY YEEEEET!"

"Yeet!" the crowd members yelled. Some of them were pumping their blocky arms up and down.

"OH AND LOOK AT THAT, ONE OF THE BEST NEW CHAMPIONS HAS ARRIVED. LADIES, GENTLEMEN, OR

WHATEVER SKIN YOU'RE WEARING, GIVE IT UP FOR GAMING NATURAL, PRO-GAMER DEAN CHINGOO2011!!!"

The crowd then noticed me at the entrance. I thought that they would crush me like a sandwich again. But this time it was different.

This time, instead of them just crushing me, they started screaming my name, cheering like crazy and saying crazy stuff like, like "Dean, marry me!", "Dean, take my robux!" and even "Dean, eat my sandwich!"

It was all weird, and it was all funny. I laughed and waved. Everything was so different now and that might have been because this was the final stadium.

I saw the other champions come. One of them was my real-life roblox friend,

Username: htkkmerg. It was very surprising.

He didn't notice me so I went up and tapped him on one blocky shoulder.

"Uh Merg? What are you doing here?" I asked.

"Hmm?" Merg saw me in surprise. "Hey, Merg, I'm Chingoo2011. I know you because this isn't my actual avatar in roblox but it's my real self."

"Oh, so do you like, um, are you going to compete in the stadium?" Merg asked.

"Yeah and we played Tower Defence Simulator before. Remember?" I asked.

"Yep," Merg replied.

We waited until all of the champions arrived. The other champions finally got there and saw us chatting. Some of them looked like big jerks, with mohawks and scars on their faces.

"Oh you are Dean the Loser?" asked one of the champions.

"Yeah, so what? Are you dumb? I am not a loser, you are," I said. I glared at his username. It was BttlMstr35.

"By the way, who taught you to spell? Your name isn't really ButtleMister35, is it?"

Merg laughed hard and the champion growled. "Oh yeah, well your name isn't really Dean Chingoo2011, is it?"

The rest of the champions stared. "Uh, yeah. That is my name."

"Oh," he said, sounding very upset. "Well, that's stupid."

"Your face is stupid," I said.

He growled again and walked away from me. I was going to enjoy destroying ButtleMister in the stadium.

Merg tapped me on the shoulder with his fingerless hand. "You know that he and whatever friends he has are going to try to gang up on you and kill you now, right?"

"It's alright. All of the matches are lvl and he's a loser. I don't care." I turned to him, face to face. "And, If they make it unfair then i won't care because i have you Merg."

"I WILL BEAT-" the champion screamed from fair a way. I cut him off.

"Yeah, not interested because you are toxic as all heck," I yelled back.

"Also we bet you have garbage towers!" Merg added.

The bully growled one more time. "My name's BattleMaster, nerd, and I'm going to crush you."

He stomped off into the locker room. The other champions and challengers started filing in behind him. We were the last to enter. Overhead we could hear the speakers booming through the ceiling.

"ALL CHAMPIONS HAVE ARRIVED!" it announced. I looked around and frowned. This was strange because one person was missing. But they said everyone was here.

"BUT IT WON'T START YET," the announcer continued. "ALL CHAMPIONS WILL BE GRANTED TIME TO PICK WHICH TOWERS THEY WANT TO CHOOSE! FOR THE NEXT FIFTEEN MINUTES THEY WILL BE ABLE TO SPEND THEIR TIME IN THE DOME PICKING TOWER AND ARMY LOADOUTS AND CHATTING IN THE LOBBY!"

"Woah, that's pretty good. I thought we'd have to start right away. Is this some kind of luxury stadium?" I asked Merg.

"I dunno man. I can say that it looks good though."

I nodded and we walked into the dome locker room, sitting in the corner to pick our towers and armies.

"Oh I have one of the best towers!" I said.

"What tower?" Merg asked.

"I have code 9801 which summons tanks. Actually my loadout is sick. I have code 9801, The Mechanical Abomination, The Lego Horde, The High-tech Bunker, and the S.W.A.T Team," I said.

"Dude, that is insane. This is my loadout".

"High-tech Bunker, Accelerating tesla, the S.W.A.T Team, the Tower Of Doom, and a normal Bunker," Merg said as he stared at my loadout because I am lucky.

"Oof if we have to fight at the end that is actually a pretty good loadout" I said.

Chapter 12 - Let the Games Being

A voice boomed over the intercom.

"ALL PLAYERS PLEASE PROCEED TO THE ARENA FOR INTRODUCTION TO THE AUDIENCE."

I looked at my friend, Merg, and I could see his blocky body shake with nervousness. I was shaking a little too. This was the last contest before I went home and it didn't look like it was going to be easy at all.

Everybody lined up and then we walked out through a tunnel into the arena. All around us sat Robloxians of every shape and color, all screaming and cheering.

I tried to look into the stands to find Jelly Janny selling her Dean Hanson merch, but she was nowhere to be found.

A golden circle appeared in the middle of the arena and one by one the players in our line stepped into it. Every time someone stepped into the circle, they gleamed and a large picture of them appeared in the sky, along with their names, and also their win and loss totals.

The first person was the bully ButtleMister35. Well, really BttlMstr35, but we all know what that means. I could see that he had seventy-four wins and twenty-six losses.

I was suddenly very scared.

I had never even played this game before, ButtTurdMister, thirty-five years old, was a definite pro. And I knew that he was going to come after me.

We kept in line, one after another, and Merg stepped into the circle. I was surprised to see that he had played two-hundred and seventy nine times!

I was even more surprised when I saw that he had won two-hundred of them. He was going to be a hard guy to beat. I hoped we wouldn't have to face each other.

When I stepped into the circle it flashed red and showed zero games won or lost.

"Hey," I yelled. "I've played a lot of games."

"NEW TO OUR GAME, BUT AN UPCOMING CHAMPION IN HIS OWN RIGHT, IT IS DEAN!"

The crowd roared in excitement and I braced myself, wondering if I was going to have to fight my way through another pack of rabid fans. But they stayed in the flying lines of stadium seating and I breathed a sigh of relief.

I walked out of the circle and stood to the side, watching the rest of the line push forward. There was someone very interesting at the very back of the line. Someone in a dark black cloak with a dark black hoodie. I kept my eye on whoever it was. They seemed like they might be trouble.

The line moved forward and at last the mysterious figure moved into the circle. At the same time, she threw back her hood.

It was Jelly Janny!

Her picture popped into the sky and the stadium screamed, all surprised and excited in the same breath. Five-hundred and one wins, the picture stated. Zero losses. Her name was embossed in gold and underneath were the words LEGENDARY.

I was shocked. My friend Jelly Janny was a legendary pro?! And I might have to fight her?!!

Oh yeah, I thought, *this is going to be just fine.* I was a little sad. I felt like I would lose easily.

But there was no choice because I needed to get back home before my parents woke up. Otherwise they would go crazy searching for me even while I was still trying to get out of here.

I needed to come up with a strat. Otherwise known as a strategy. A plan used for being smart at playing games, board games, or even challenges. I really needed to get out of here so I could go find mom and dad. I hoped very much that they weren't awake yet.

And I was scared that if I lost then I would need to get robux by working as a janitor. Then I would have to start over with all of the stadiums.

And if I lost again then I would have to repeat it over and over again like that kid from the Fairyland book who went crazy because she couldn't finish her quest. I didn't want to become a crazy gangster like her.

So I needed to win.

I looked around me. I needed to see what map I would be playing on, what the terrain looked like, and lastly I needed to find out where the HQs would be and how long the roads were to them.

A bunch of spinning game wheels appeared in the sky. They sounded like sound blades, which totally made me cringe. All of us competitors watched, hoping to be paired with the weakest among us. Which I figured was probably the player named SillyBilly1329 because when he had appeared in the line up almost all of his plays had been losses.

"Please be Silly Billy," I muttered, over and over. "I swear, if Silly Billy plays me, I will never ever forget to do my homework ever again. Well, sometimes."

The wheels were spinning and ticking slower by the second. Finally they stopped. My rectangular Roblox jaw dropped. I would be battling against Sir Buttle Mister the 35th, the biggest butthead in the whole universe.

I turned my head and we locked eyes. And stared. My head raced with thoughts and ideas.

Winning is part of losing and losing is part of winning. In order to win I would need to figure out not only what is best, but also what is worst. If I didn't recognize possible mistakes, I would lose quickly. So I would have to plan accordingly.

The best defense is the best offense. That meant that I would need to focus on making a good defense. But at the same time I would need to save a lot of money for a boss rush, or a rush of powerful units all at the same time.

This would let me overwhelm Buttface Mister's defenses and destroy his HQ.

It would be a matter of balance because I had to spend just enough money to stop his forces but at the same time be able to save enough money to be ready to mass produce my own.

If I made any mistakes with my defenses, I would probably lose.

BttlMstr35 laughed and turned his head away, breaking eye contact. Was that a good thing, or a bad thing?

I didn't know.

Tunnels opened up with all of our names on them and I headed over to the tunnel for my coming match. I was scared. I had a good strategy but was it good enough? I just hoped that he was dumb enough to fall to my trap.

The crowd started splitting up and thinning as each of the competitors moved away towards their own tunnels. Now it was just me and BttlMstr35. We walked together to the battle. He glanced at me with deadly eyes. I met his eyes and didn't flinch, making sure not to move one blocky muscle on my blocky face.

When the match started I would first place something cheap and good. The highest defense I could. I'd wait to place anything until his first units entered my territory and make it an ambush. That way I could choose exactly the right type of defensive units to counter what he sent.

And just in case things went wrong I figured I'd also purchase the level one HP upgrade as soon as I could.

We were walking through the tunnel now and we could both see that it was a winter map full of frozen roads drifting over with a wash of unplowed snow. A notification appeared before the zone.

WELCOME TO WINTERLAND. ALL ICE CORE UNITS HAVE THEIR HITPOINTS DOUBLED HERE. ALL FIRE CORE UNITS HAVE THEIR HITPOINTS HALVED. BUT FIRE UNITS WILL DO TRIPLE DAMAGE ON THIS MAP.

And then my plan hit me. I'd ambush the first wave of attacks with fire units, follow them with the slowest and tankiest ice units I could to delay his advance and make him angry.

When he was angry he would buy too many units, and while I was keeping him back I could upgrade my income so that I would build money up more quickly than he did. And with that bit of planning, I was ready to fight a pro.

Chapter 13 - The First Round Of Luck Or Skill

It was time. I had no choice but to face him. BttlMstr35 had walked across the way and he was now on the opposite side of the battlefield. It was time to see who was the better player.

I was going to win. I could feel it in my heart, beating hard and fast. I was going to win because there was no other option. I was going to get home to see mom and dad.

"Good luck Dean," BttlMstr35 yelled from the top of a tower, across the fields of snow and the roads snaking through the land. We were both in towers, watching our money rise and viewing the battlefield, waiting to place attack bases and defensive units.

"Why would you say that," I asked. "You're a jerk. And ugly."

"Because you are going to need it to defeat me. Taunt me all that you want to," he said. "I am level 127 in this game, and you are just a noob. I am going to win."

"Here's the thing," I yelled. "I am not just the avatar of someone. I'm not a Robloxian either. I'm a real person, here in the game, and that is going to give me the advantage because I can see things in ways that none of you can see them."

He paused, his face all scrunched up in Roblox madness.

"That's not right. You are lying!" he said.

I shrugged my shoulders. "Well, ask yourself if I really am and if it makes a difference. I think you are underestimating me. Because let me tell you a secret. I can beat you because you won't be careful. And I will because I have too much on the line for me to fail"

"THE FIRST ROUND SHALL BEGIN!" the announcer said.

Folks cheered like a megaphone.

"Here goes nothing." I said.

I watched my money rise and saw BttlMster place two scout units right at the entrance to his lands.

I placed a production unit of my own, but just a single medieval barracks. I could afford two of them, but I needed to keep him from getting suspicious so I had to keep occasionally buying while upgrading my income and preparing for the big rush.

Also, the barracks was a bit of a trick. After it got enough experience points, I could upgrade it to a gunpowder barracks, a bunker, then a high-tech bunker.

It was a bit of an investment, since the last upgrade cost a lot of money besides. But the units there were cyborg assault troopers who fired lasers and used electric whips for their melee attacks.

Both were quite powerful.

After the barracks was placed, units started spawning and emerging, then rushing over the roads towards the enemy's HQ. BttlMstr35 laughed.

"Do you really think that one barracks can generate enough units to defeat me?"

I nodded and said nothing, but tried to look scared. He laughed again, even while I upgraded my income. His scouts pounded at my rushing, bearded berserkers who piled out from the thatched bunker cottages straight into the trained rifles of the scout platoons.

"Like shooting fish in a barrel," BttlMstr said, laughing some more. "I'm not even breaking a sweat.

He upgraded his scouts to rangers, I saw, their tactical gear morphing into more state of the art stuff, their aim zeroing in, their faces and bodies growing more muscular.

Behind them he set up more scout platoons.

Meanwhile I upgraded my income again. It was beginning to pour in. I set up another medieval barracks and tossed out a bunch of my own scouts.

They were a generic unit, but also very cost-effective ones, so they were perfect for my plan. He narrowed his eyes.

"Do you really think your vikings there can do anything to me? You are dumber than you look."

I had to be careful. His rangers leveled to star commandos and they were now lasering my poor vikings in half.

"To Valhalla!" one screamed before exploding into dust a moment later.

And then he pulled out his chosen unit selection. Zombie specialty. My jaw dropped. I had expected him to go with Frost! He saw my shock and pumped a fist into the air. He knew he was going to win.

"Defend against this," he yelled.

First came the virals, super fast runners that did a fair amount of damage. They tore into the vikings in their path while my scouts popped off their heads with their rifles.

Behind them, though, came the heavy maulers, brutal hulk type zombies who had tons of hitpoints and did tremendous damage. I was nervous. I'd grabbed some flame types for my deck, but I hadn't grabbed any electric types.

I paused, my eyes wide. There was an electric type. A very powerful electric type.

The only one I had.

If I upgraded the barracks to their top level, the cyborg assault troopers they produced would have an incredible electric melee attack. And electric melee attacks did double damage to zombies!

I stared as he filled the roads of his lands with zombie hordes, going for a rush attack.

As if I were a zombie myself I rolled through all of my barracks, upgraded them to their max, then pounded out four more barracks behind them, spending all of my money.

It was my turn to laugh. I saw that, with all of my money spent on units and all of his money spent on units, our armies were equally valuable.

But I had upgraded my income several times. It meant that from this point on I was going to be able to outspend him!

I waved at him.

"Hey dummy, looks like you used all of your money," I said.

He growled, staring at the battle down below. The weak viking units had been chewed up and torn to bits by the zombies, and they were rising from the roadway as zombies themselves.

They were no match for my marching cyborgs, however. Their lasers hurt them a lot from a distance, but it was their electric whips that really did the trick.

And best of all, when the zombies clumped together too much, the shock attacks traveled through the whole bunch of them, doing extra damage to all of them.

"What?" BttlMstr finally asked. "Why? Why wouldn't you go with an all-flame deck in this sort of map?"

"Dude, I didn't even know we could know what types of maps we were going to be playing on. You see, I chose this deck not just because it is good. I chose this deck because I didn't know, and because, like you said, I am a noob."

"You dumb idiot," he whined.

All around us the crowd started booing him. I saw some people wearing his merch get up and start walking out. I also saw people wearing Dean merch start to throw trash in his direction.

A green forcefield flared up, disintegrating the junk.

"Looks like this dumb idiot just lost you some fans," I said.

On the battlefield my berserkers from the new barracks were getting torn apart, but I was able to upgrade them to gunpowder arquebusiers, bearded men with triangular helms firing guns shaped like horns.

Not a great upgrade, but they were lasting longer and soon they'd have enough xps and I'd have enough money to upgrade them again.

On his side BttlMstr upgraded his zombies and I saw them get bigger and stronger. But we could both see that on the battlefield it wasn't making much of a difference.

In fact, given how the battle had turned, BttlMstr's final focus on his offensive zombie armies were what ended him.

Offensive units can't attack defensive units since they are off of the road, and if he had focused on defensive units I'd have had to wade through them taking damage all the while.

Instead my armies tore apart his zombies, taking some damage on the way, but punching through to attack the base of his tower.

"No. No!" he yelled. His tower blazed and sparked, at 50 hp, then 10, and then it crumbled.

"DEAN WINS! VICTORY!"

"That's not possible," BttlMstr screamed, falling with the rock of his tower. He plowed into the muddy snow below.

"BAN THAT CHEATER NOW! I WON AND HE LOST. HE IS PLAYING

UNFAIRLY SO BAN HIM NOW!" he said.

All around the crowd was chanting. "Dean! Dean! Dean!"

"SIR, YOU HAVE LOST AND DEAN WAS PLAYING FAIRLY BY PLAYING SMART." the announcer said.

"WELL. ASK THE CROWD!" he said angrily.

"You lost! You didn't win and you are very loud! Dean won fair and square!, yeah!" the crowd shouted.

I smiled up at the cloudy Roblox sky. One down, four more to go. And, maybe, a fight with my friend Jelly Janny as well!

Chapter 14 - Battle Montage

The next three rounds were very difficult.

In my second matchup I faced against an opponent who had taken a Lawful - Elven loadout and I could see right away why he had done that.

The shiny armored warriors started strong and even though their sylvan outposts were expensive, those bases upgraded at a decent cost and produced wonderful units at each level.

Their top tier was a mighty paladin atop a powerful and fast warhorse, a veritable juggernaut that had a very mighty sword, exceptional armor, and the ability to overrun leading units to attack those behind them.

Her name was Silvia17 and she was a crafty player.

I played hard and tried to trick her again using my income increases, but she was hoarding me hard from the start and I had to keep building defenses and barracks.

Luckily I had the Lego Horde, and it turned out to be not just a powerful attack against the paladins, but also a hilarious one. The little plastic men charged forward and whenever a horse stepped on one of them it squealed in pain and faded on the spot.

It was the perfect counter, and between them and my cyborgs, I won the round.

In the third round, I had to fight a person whose clothes and body were pitch black. A mysterious figure who had named himself DARKMASTER527.

He was a unique challenge because his loadout was so random and chaotic.

Some units were from old times, others were from imaginative and unknown places. I had planned to save my money and upgrade my income again, but he started off the match with a ballet dojo, flooding my borders with the leaping sword-wielding nightmares known as ninja ballerinas.

I fought back by placing a lego horde, a very different strategy from what I had been doing before because this one was not thought out at all.

The lego fountain was cheap, and the xp level up markers were low, so I maxed it out quickly. Lego horde after lego horde were kicked off into space by the screaming ballerinas, but they were kept the border safe.

Now I was able to upgrade my money production. But as if he had been waiting for that moment, he placed a bunch of cemeteries onto his lot, sending forward a wave of zombies.

He made it about halfway to my HQ before I was able to counter with a smattering of barracks placements and upgrades, getting out my cyborg warriors.

Unlike the others, it was a battle of attrition. His bases grew in number, as did mine, and we both upgraded our incomes.

The audience grew quiet and tense. Who could win such a long-standing battle?

As the hordes battled, we both sat back and let our incomes grow. It was time to settle the fight with a boss battle.

DARKMASTER527 went first, placing a large and ancient treant with massive hitpoints and attack damage, but slow movement speed.

The audience held their breath.

This old-fashioned boss type was very powerful and immune to a lot of damage types as well.

But I smiled. Because I had the perfect counter. And it wasn't even a boss.

It was the Mechanical Abomination.

I placed the Mechanical Abomination. It was a factory that made mechs. And leveled to the max, the mechs it made were for mass destruction and chaos, equipped with buzz saws for melee attack and plasma rifles for ranged battle.

It was the perfect counter.

As the first little mechs sauntered out to get annihilated by DARKMASTER's forces, I got experience points and, using those and my saved income, I leveled them up to the max.

The factories shifted production, grinding and chugging loudly as they started spawning little deadly mechs.

And to top it off, at max level, there was a Mechanical Abomination leader mech in every wave of 100 regular mechs. These towered over the others, mini-bosses in their own right.

DARKMASTER howled as his Treant swept the front line of cyber soldiers and lego, only to be ground down and set on fire by the marauding mech warriors.

The audience cheered, waving and clapping.

Not long after the amazing comeback encounter, I was victorious.The third round was down. Still 2 to go.

But then I had to face up with Merg. I was sad having to see myself fighting against Merg. But I had no choice. It had already been chosen the way it should have been.

"Hey Merg." I said.

"Hey Dean. It sucks to be in this position, he said.

"Well I guess we have to fight," I said.

And we went through our tunnels facing each other. This was going to end badly as both of us had a chance to win.

After we chose our sides I placed the same tower again. A Medieval barracks. And after that I upgraded my money production. Then I started scouting.

I saw some normal zombies approaching slowly. Then I got the money for more money production. I clicked it and money came in decently quickly. But then I bought 4 more barracks because I had the money and for protection.

Merg didn't seem to like what he had seen. I saw him put some money into defenses and some into sending waves of zombies to protect his base.

Merg sending zombies actually did a great job cleaning out my barbarians. In fact it made it so that it was harder for me to defend. But waves passed by and I upgraded my money production more and more.

I upgraded my 5 barracks to level 2. And it had spawned arquebusiers. It meant that I could shoot from a long distance.

But these guns weren't that good. Arquebuses had almost zero accuracy until just a few feet away, so my units shot and shot, throwing up big clouds of dry black dust without doing much damage.

Still, closer in, they were devastating! The zombies and arquebusiers battled back and forth, and control of the road between us wavered.

After several waves, I was able to upgrade my money production. So I maxed all five of my barracks, creating my feared cyborg assault units and destroying all of the zombies in my way.

Merg palmed his face into a blocky hand as his HQ exploded and crumbled around him.

"Good game!" he yelled from across the way.

I had won but it was a sad victory. To win I'd had to fight against one of my dearest friends. It was a win that felt hollow. I hoped he wouldn't hate me now.

I got down and walked over to him, expecting the worst. Merg walked towards me as well, his face unreadable.

Then, at the last moment, he laughed and ran forward, wrapping me in a hug.

"Super good game. I was going to let you win, but it turns out I didn't have to. You are really good at this!" he said and he did a little kick dance.

I joined him, laughing now. I was almost home. There was just one more round.

Chapter 15 - A Battle to the Finish

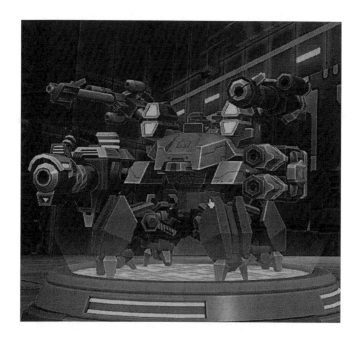

When Merg and I walked out of our battle stadium, I saw that the other match was still in progress. But it wouldn't be for long.

We settled into the locker room to watch the game on TV. There we could see Jelly Janny dancing in her tower, her units slowly pushing back those of her opponent.

She had gone with a food-based loadout, and her side of the map was filled with waffle-makers, sandwich-makers, and frying pans that produced a bunch of slow-moving, butter-and-syrup-covered waffles, PB and J sandwiches, and steaks.

The units wobbled as they walked, and they didn't fight well. They were weird and I looked closely, trying to see what was the plan.

And then I saw it. They weren't meant to be good fighting units. Her enemy, HmsterRick, was using an Orcish loadout, and the strong, meaty warriors were in heaven. They run into a food mob then tear it apart, feasting upon the enemy units, falling back under the barrage of deliciousness.

Orc chieftains lay moaning on the road, their faces sticky with syrup and butter, their hands stained with steak juice and their bellies sticking out like basketballs.

"No more," an orcish warrior moaned, before burping hard, long and loud like my dad.

"Please stop," cried another.

I was surprised. One, I didn't know that units could talk like that.

And two, I had no idea about food-based units.

Could I even fight them? I was very worried. Those orcs looked tough and they had brought HmsterRick up this far.

Yet Jelly was clearly going to win.

Was I doomed to failure?

The fight finally finished when JellyJanny conjured up a gigantic birthday cake boss covered in multiple layers of frosting. The orcs shook and moaned, rolling and diving off the path, letting the cake stomp through and hit HmsterRick's tower.

The cake charged at the last moment, exploding all over the tower and knocking it over, 0 hps left. Jelly Janny had won.

I felt good for my friend. But not good for myself. I had fought four rounds. And I was so close to being home. I couldn't lose. Not now.

I left the locker room just in time to see Jelly come out of the stadium, trailed by a frosty cake monster that was surely HmsterRick.

Jelly locked eyes with me and smiled, her block hand raised up in a wave. I waved back. Everyone started cheering.

"WELL, FOLKS, IT IS TIME FOR AN INTERLUDE. THE CHAMPIONSHIP FIGHT WILL START IN TWENTY MINUTES. NEWCOMER PRO CHINGOO2011 VS REIGNING CHAMPION, JELLYJANNY!"

The scream continued, people yelling for me and for her, and I saw people leaning forward as we got closer to each other.

I think they thought we were going to do some smack talk or say bad things to each other. I ignored them, focusing on my friend.

"I'm impressed Dean. You managed to get through all four rounds without losing," Jelly said. She wrapped me up in a big hug.

"Yeah but it was challenging," I replied.

She put a hand on both of my shoulders. "Everything worth anything is challenging. And it should be. If it was easy, then it wouldn't be worth it. Right?"

I grumbled a little. "Yeah, I guess. But some things are more than that. Some things are more than worth it. They are needed! Like my mom and my dad."

JellyJanny nodded. "I'd lose on purpose if I could," she whispered. "But I can't lie to my fans. Plus, if I get caught throwing the match, I will be banned from Roblox. But, Dean, you can win. I believe in you."

Jelly pulled away from me and turned to the crowd. "Oh, Chingoo2011, you think you are so tough. Well, then, you should be able to fight me. And win."

I was confused. What was she doing now? "Umm, yeah, maybe I will!"

The crowd started chanting. "Jelly Ching, Jelly Ching, Jelly Ching."

"Hear that Ching-a-ling? My name first. I'm undefeatable. And the crowd knows it."

I chuckled. She was playing up the crowd. I could see JellyJanny and Dean merch being pushed by Robloxians through the rows and columns of spectators.

"All undefeated really means is hasn't faced Chingoo2011."

The crowd roared.

"ARE WE READY FOR THE FINAL ROUND, ROUND FIVE?!" the announcer shouted.

Had it been twenty minutes already? The crowds cheered and laughed, nomnomnoming hotdogs and soft drinks. The sound was deafening, so much so that I knew no one could hear our final exchange.

"I mean it, Dean. I can't go easy on you, but I believe in you. Good luck!"

"Thanks Jelly!" I said. We made our way into the stadium, saying nothing else. We cleared our minds, thinking up battle strategies and preparing for the worst.

The final match had a new map, titled Major Carnage. It looked like the Colosseum from Rome, and the modifiers were all different.

Now frozen units had nine times as many hitpoints and fire enemies did four times as much damage.

The common unit loadout had been replaced, so all of the regular units that both of us could produce were changed.

I felt panic set in.

Freeze Zombies, Fire Imps, Lava Mephits?!

I didn't know anything about them, not really. I hoped against hope I wouldn't need them, and that I could win using my chosen loadout.

I started off the round by placing a barracks to protect my road, and to prompt her to respond.

She just waited, letting my Vikings wander into her territory and get near her tower before she spawned a flame pit, letting fire imps jump out and set the Vikings on fire.

They beat the Vikings and pushed forward, fighting and defeating another and another wave of my Viking friends.

I felt scared, but I refused to put down another barracks, instead upgrading my money production. She placed another fire pit and I responded by upgrading my first barracks, producing arquebusiers.

Those guys, I was surprised and happy to see, blasted the fire imps into pieces at close range.

Jelly set up a frying pan and I quickly found that the arquebusiers were tenderizing the steaks before sitting down to eat them.

I needed something different for that one. So I set up a S.W.A.T. station, letting the armored vans ram into the steaks and push them back.

Things looked good for me as a few waves passed. But she finally responded to the S.W.A.T. vans with freeze zombies, slow giants that cracked and crushed my vans with their crinkling limbs.

I upgraded my money production again, then placed four more barracks. I'd need to level these up and get to my cyborgs so I could wipe out the freeze zombies, because at times nine hitpoints they were almost impossible to kill.

Flame imps, vikings, arquebusiers, steaks, S.W.A.T. and freeze zombies battled hard along the roadside, pushing back and forth.

More rounds passed by and the crowd hushed. It looked like we might be at a tie. I looked at the flame imps and put out some freeze zombies of my own.

She countered with Auto-Turrets, defense towers with high caliber, high fire capabilities that tore the slow movers to shreds.

I checked the combat menu, found the Auto-Turrets, and set up some of my own. The minutes ticked by, the whole battlefield becoming a giant burning and frozen mess.

I upgraded again and again.

She did as well.

Steaks became giant triple cheeseburgers. Zombies became Ice Yetis. S.W.A.T. became battle tanks.

Explosions rocked the arena even while the crisp, delicious smell of greasy burger meat wafted through and tripled food sales in the audience.

Her forces were pushing me back. Slowly my units were failing. I waited and Jelly looked confused from across the battlefield.

"Why aren't you building more units or upgrading your bases?" she asked from atop her tower.

"Great advice," I responded.

And I used my built-up income to place my Mechanical Abomination.

Little mechs poured out and started to blast apart Jelly's giant horde. I saw her panic, spending her own money on a series of giant cake bosses.

She made ten of them. I was in trouble.

The cakes overfed my regular troops, swamped my tanks and mechs, and were generally making a giant mess of things on the ground.

But the xps were rolling in and I quickly maxed my Mechanical Abomination, allowing for the advanced mech squads with mini bosses to roll out and do their work.

Plasma blasted, saw blades rumbled, and my mechanical army with the mechanical leader rushed the horde doing their best to stop them from entering.

Cyborgs, mechs, zombies and tanks shot their miniguns, shot their missiles, even called for reinforcements, and kept resisting until they had to retreat because of all of the attempts to kill the major bosses.

Broken and smashed units lay everywhere. The barracks had been maxed, but it wasn't enough.

I looked across the way and saw that it had been Jelly's plan all along. Her eyes shined sorry even as her soldiers beat down my forces in front of my tower.

My HQ only had ten hitpoints while Jelly's was still at one-hundred hitpoints.

But I knew something she didn't.

I knew that I had been losing the war, letting her push in, because I had stopped spending.

"Looks like it's game over. You need to try better next time," she said.

"Nope," I replied. "I'm going full power."

I opened the combat menu and pushed the nuke button, spending half of my money on it.

A mushroom cloud soared and a storm of atomic energy surged out, destroying all of my and Jelly's armies and defenses.

I used the second half of the money I had been saving to spawn the Mega GMSG. It was a giant robot capable of destroying cities and only spawnable with the Mechanical Abomination fully leveled.

The gigantic mech stomped forward, very sharp points at the end of its legs stabbing through new unit spawns as it tread through to Jelly's tower.

Jelly spawned a gigantic cyclops and watched in dismay as it was blasted away by my boss unit's Photon Cannon. It led the way as another army of mechs were following it from behind.

Jelly was shocked.

She placed all of the defenses she could afford. But she'd spent too much money on her last offensive, so now she simply didn't have enough to resist my advance.

Jelly waved her arms at me, catching my attention. "How?" she asked, her face scrunched up in awe.

"Mega GMSG. The most expensive unit you can spawn," I said.

As her tower exploded into flame and smoke, she smiled and turned to the audience. "Let's hear it for Dean!"

The crowd cheered and yelled. Then I saw that Jelly's HQ had fallen. The final round had been won by me.

Chapter 16 - The Big Finale

Just as I came down from my tower, the crowd cheered so loud that I needed to cover my ears. My fans and the Dean merch people were screaming. It had been the loudest day EVER in my life!

Across the battlefield came Jelly, pumping her blocky Roblox legs as fast as she could. I started running too, and we met in the middle with a big old Roblox thud, falling to the ground, dizzy.

Jelly was the first one to get up. "Dean, that was amazing! I know I said I believed in you but, you know, I was like ninety-five percent sure I was going to win."

"Hey!" I yelled, laughing. I knew she was kidding.

"Alright, maybe just ninety percent." Her eyes widened. "For a moment there I really thought you were going to lose."

"Yeah, that was a close one," I said. She grabbed my boxy hand with her own and we walked out of the stadium together.

"LADIES AND GENTLEBLOX, I CANNOT BELIEVE WHAT WE HAVE JUST SEEN HERE TONIGHT. THE UPSTART NEWCOMER

DESTROYING THE REIGNING CHAMP IN WHAT CAN ONLY BE DESCRIBED AS THE BIGGEST UPSET IN HISTORY. SAY HELLO TO THE NEW WORLD CHAMPION, CHINGOO2011!"

Jelly pulled my hand up, showing the audience. They cheered and laughed and hugged. Roses were thrown all around me, disappearing as soon as they touched the ground. I bowed to my left and to my right.

"Jelly, this is a bit too much. Can we get out of here?" I asked.

Together we ran to the locker rooms, the cheers of the crowd fading behind us.

We sat on a wooden bench, silent, still holding hands. Then Jelly turned and looked me in the eyes, her other hand finding my free one.

"Now you can go home, Dean," she said. Her voice was quiet, with a little shake to it, and her eyes were shiny, like two puddles on a sunlit summer day.

"Hey, don't be sad, Jelly. You knew that I would have to go home. My mom and dad will be worried if I'm not there when they wake up. Plus, this isn't my world."

She nodded and turned her head away. I wasn't sure what to do. She looked miserable, a person overcome with complete sadness, and I'd never had any experience with anything like that before.

She coughed and cleared her throat.

"Are you ever going to come back?" she asked me.

I looked down at the long row of boxes that showed me my inventory and saw all the robux I had made. Enough to get me home a thousand times if I needed to.

"Of course I am. And you and me, we are going to have the time of our lives!"

The End?

AFTERWORD

Thanks for reading my book.
If you like it please leave me a review!
Here is a picture of my teddy sheep, Chingoo! He was the first of my many teddy animals and he is the pet that I get in my book!

ABOUT THE AUTHOR
Dean Hanson

Dean is a ten year old kid who loves Nerf Guns, Legos, Computer Games and Youtube. He is very creative and he likes to make stories as well as design new things. He hopes to grow up to become an architect.

Dean loves to gab and play games and you can find him (sometimes with his dad) on Roblox. His name is Chingoo2011 and he looks forward to meeting you.

Wanna find some more good books? Come check out our site at
https://damienhansonbooks.com/

Or check out some of our affiliates at
https://dameshandsome.com/
Dames Handsome
https://www.facebook.com/DamesHandsome
LitRPG Forum
https://www.facebook.com/groups/litrpgforum
LitRPG Books
https://www.facebook.com/groups/LitRPG.books
Kids GameLit
https://www.facebook.com/groups/kidslitrpg
LitRPG Legends
https://www.facebook.com/groups/litrpglegends
GameLitSociety @
https://www.facebook.com/groups/LitRPGsociety/

To learn more about LitRPG, talk to authors including myself, and just have an awesome time, please join the LitRPG Group.

Made in the USA
Monee, IL
01 October 2023